BELVA LOCKWOOD
WINS HER CASE

Belva A. Lockwood

When Belva argued a case, she would have looked like this.

BELVA LOCKWOOD WINS HER CASE

Drollene P. Brown

Illustrated by James Watling

J
B
LOCKWOOD,
B.
c.1

Albert Whitman & Company
Niles, Illinois

"Has God given one half of his creatures talents and gifts that are but as a mockery—wings but not to fly?"
—Belva Lockwood

To my parents, Evelyn and Wilson Plattner, who have always believed, as Belva did, that the answer to that question is a resounding "Nay!"

Library of Congress Cataloging-in-Publication Data

Brown, Drollene P.
    Belva Lockwood wins her case.

    Summary: Describes the struggles and triumphs of
Belva Lockwood, the teacher, suffragette, lawyer,
and peace activist who became the first woman to
practice law before the Supreme Court and a candidate
for president in 1884 and 1888.
    1. Lockwood, Belva Ann, 1830-1917—Juvenile
literature. 2. Lawyers—United States—Biography—
Juvenile literature. 3. Women lawyers—United
States—Biography—Juvenile literature. [1. Lockwood,
Belva Ann, 1830-1917. 2. Lawyers. 3. Women lawyers]
I. Watling, James, ill. II. Title.
KF368.L58B76 1987   349.73'092'4 [B] [92] 87-2114
                          347.300924 [B]
ISBN 0-8075-0630-3 (lib. bdg.)

Text © 1987 by Drollene P. Brown
Illustrations © 1987 by James Watling
Published in 1987 by Albert Whitman & Company, Niles, Illinois
Published simultaneously in Canada by General Publishing, Limited, Toronto
10 9 8 7 6 5 4 3 2 1

Contents

1 The Girl Who Wanted to Move Mountains

Belva backed out of the little pond on her parents' farm. Her pantalets were dripping wet, and her skirt was edged with mud. As she listened to her shoes squish, she shook her head in surprise.

Her mother was surprised, too. She didn't understand why her ten-year-old daughter would do anything so foolish as try to walk on water. But Belva Ann Bennett went to church regularly with her parents, and she believed that anything that could be done in Bible times could be done in her time.

Belva had been born in a log cabin in Royalton, Niagara County, New York, on October 24, 1830. Her parents, Hannah Green and Lewis J. Bennett, had been born in Washington County, New York, but they lived in Royalton when they married in December 1827. At the time of their marriage, Hannah was fifteen years old, and Lewis was twenty. The following September, their first daughter, Rachel, was born. Belva was their second child. There were three others: Warren, the only boy, born in 1832; Cyrene, born in 1834; and Inverno, born in 1841.

Like other family farms, the Bennett farm had enough chores for everyone. The crops in that area were primarily fruit trees, but each farm had its own vegetable garden, chickens, and cows. Lewis Bennett grew apples, pears, peaches, and plums for market.

Belva liked living on the farm. She could walk along the top of a fence for a mile or more, and one of her favorite chores was riding a farm horse, bareback, to bring in the cows. In later years, Belva remembered not being afraid of snakes or spiders or anything else, and she said her face was very often dirty. In other words, she was hardly the picture of a prim Victorian Age "little lady."

The country girl enjoyed school, too. From the time she was five, she had walked to school with her big sister, Rachel. All the children there, from the youngest five-year-old to the oldest fourteen-year-old, studied in the same room and had to recite lessons each day. There was a white line painted or chalked on the floor, and the child, when standing to recite, had to "toe the mark." Older girls and boys helped the younger ones with their lessons. Sometimes the teacher was a fifteen-year-old who had been reciting at the chalked line only a year before.

The youngest children couldn't go to school in the winter, for the snows were too deep and the storms too dangerous to allow little ones to walk safely. Although she often had to miss school, Belva became an enthusiastic student and a good reader. By the time she was ten, she had read the entire Bible through, and she believed every word of it.

She thought about her inability to walk on water. Perhaps she had failed because she was doing it only for fun. Belva looked for a more serious test of her faith. A little girl on a nearby farm had died recently. How glorious it would be for the parents if they had their daughter back, she thought. But no matter how much she concentrated, she couldn't bring the child back to life.

Still, Belva wasn't ready to give up. Maybe she should start with something small. She had read in her Bible that a person with as much faith as a very tiny seed can move mountains with that faith alone. Her past experience had shown that she probably didn't have that much faith. But surely she could move a little hill. Belva selected a dome of land and sat down across from it. She thought very hard. Not a pebble tumbled. She concentrated with all her might. Not even a breeze stirred. She didn't think of anything except that hill. It didn't budge.

She saw that faith wasn't enough. If she really wanted that hill moved, she'd have to do it one shovelful at a time.

2 Out in the World

When Belva was fourteen, her father believed it was time for her to contribute more to the household. She had finished eight grades—the only ones for which free schooling was available—and it was now proper for her to settle down, help her mother at home, and await the time when she would marry. Like many other people in those days, Lewis Bennett believed that girls did not need to go to school beyond the eighth grade. Too much schooling, it was thought, would turn the girls into "old maids."

But Belva wanted more education, and her mother sided with her. Although Hannah had never gone to school, she saw how important learning was to her daughter. Reluctantly, Lewis agreed to allow his daughter more school if she could earn the money for it. The farm supported the family, but there was no extra money for "frills" such as higher education.

One morning, a determined fourteen-year-old walked to Royalton for a meeting with the five trustees of the village. They were considering applicants for teaching summer school. This special session was held not only for young children who couldn't attend in the winter but also for farm boys who had missed school during spring planting and fall harvesting. Belva got the job.

Teaching rough farm boys would have frightened most fourteen-year-old girls, but Belva had a goal in mind. When she started some task, she always believed she would succeed. One can imagine her staring down a boy who towered over her, making him "toe the mark."

Her weekly pay was five dollars. She saved every penny she could, and by the end of the summer, she had saved enough for a year's tuition at Girls' Academy in Royalton.

The school was in a large two-story brick building. It had been established for instruction in both elementary and higher branches of "English and classical education," according to advertisements in the *Niagara Democrat*, a regional newspaper.

Belva paid for most of her room and meals by doing housekeeping chores at her boardinghouse near the academy. For two more summers, she taught school to earn tuition. Each summer her salary was raised a dollar per week. Lewis Bennett wasn't happy that his grown daughter was attending school, but Hannah was proud of her second child.

Although Belva was working hard, she also had a social life. A young farmer named Uriah McNall came to visit. He called her "Bell." They fell in love, and by the time Belva graduated from Girls' Academy in May 1848, Uriah had proposed marriage. When he formally asked Belva's father for her hand, Lewis was probably relieved. The daughter who wanted higher education would have a husband, after all.

The young couple were married in Royalton on November 8, 1848. They moved to nearby Gasport, to a farm cottage that had been Uriah's home before the wedding. Gasport was much bigger than Royalton, and it was still growing. Many buildings smelled of fresh wood. Because each store was built according to the taste and peculiar notion of its owner, the doorsteps were at different levels. As a result, the wooden sidewalk along Main Street rose and fell like a series of waves.

In addition to running his farm, Uriah operated a sawmill, where logs were sawed into boards. Belva helped him. She told a reporter years later that she had "measured up many a thousand feet of lumber." She also used to sell livestock and produce for Uriah when he was away on business. Like other farm wives, she spent much of her time gardening, cooking, preserving, sewing, and doing laundry by hand.

Soon she also had a baby to tend, for Lura McNall was born on July 31, 1849. The child was toddling before she was a year old, and her parents were proud of her quickness.

By marrying Uriah, Belva was doing what was expected of girls her age.

But in addition, she continued to do what was not expected. She kept studying. She also wrote articles for the local newspaper and for literary magazines. Some of her contributions were poems to comfort those who had had a death in the family. One printed in the *Lockport Daily Journal* on November 12, 1851, reads: "Weep not, Mother, for the loved one / That so soon has passed away / Has left a world of sorrow, / For a bright and glorious day."

Before Lura's second birthday, something terrible happened. Uriah caught his foot in the sawmill machinery and was trapped under falling logs. He was carried home, limp and pale.

Uriah was unconscious for two days. At first, Belva watched over her husband fearfully. She cried for hours and ate very little. Years afterward, she wrote that this was the last time she completely lost control of her emotions. Slowly, she pulled herself out of her despair and vowed to help herself and her little family. As a teenager, Belva had taught boys who were larger and older than she. She had worked and saved her money so that she could go further in school. She had run a farm household and sold produce and livestock. Belva knew that with resolve, she could do anything that must be done. She would manage the farm, keep the sawmill going, and nurse her husband back to health.

Uriah's broken bones healed, but his inner strength seemed to have been crushed by the logs. (In later years, some members of his family guessed that he may have had tuberculosis.) After a few months of resting, he began to do small chores around the house. Then he returned to the mill, even though he tired easily.

But Uriah's step became slower, and he spent more and more time in a darkened room. On April 8, 1853, Uriah died in his sleep. He was only twenty-eight.

What was Belva to do? She was twenty-two years old, with a three-year-old daughter to care for. She would have to make her way in life without a husband's love and support. The young widow must have felt frightened and lonely.

3 Moving Little Hills

Belva couldn't have felt lonely for very long. Within a few months after Uriah's death, his brother James, Belva's brother Warren, and her sister Cyrene had moved in to board with her. The McNall farm was close to Gasport Academy, where all three were enrolled for the fall term.

The money and assistance which James, Warren, and Cyrene exchanged for board helped Lura and Belva. But Belva also took steps to help herself. She went to Royalton to visit the trustees, just as she had eight years earlier. With the same determination, she asked for a teaching job—not for summer school this time, but for a regular position in the district school. This time she had her diploma from Girls' Academy.

The trustees readily agreed to hire Belva—at a salary of seven dollars per week. But this was the same amount she had made in the final year of her summer school teaching. Now she had both experience and a diploma, and the job carried more responsibility than summer school. Men made between ten and fifteen dollars per week for the same work. Belva turned down the trustees' offer.

Shocked and angry, she went to see a friend who was the wife of the

Methodist minister. Belva explained what had happened and asked for her assistance and advice.

"I cannot help you," said the kindly woman. "You cannot help yourself. It is the way of the world."

Belva wrote later that this answer opened her eyes and "raised her dander." Here was another mountain that wouldn't go away with wishing. But she was determined to move it. The tool she needed was education.

From her study of history, Belva believed that many of the nation's great men had received a college education. Perhaps if women could learn and study as men did, they, too, could accomplish important things. Also, if women could go to college, perhaps men would value their work more.

She knew most of the nation's colleges were closed to women, but there were some that would accept female students. Belva decided to enter Gasport Academy with her boarders. She probably wanted to brush up on subjects she had studied at Girls' Academy so she would be fully prepared for a higher education.

After a year at Gasport Academy, Belva felt ready to go away to a more advanced school. But how could she be a student all day in a strange place and still take care of her little girl? Hannah, always sympathetic to her second daughter's ambition for higher education, offered to keep Lura while Belva went to Genesee Wesleyan Seminary in Lima, New York. This school wasn't a college, but it was more advanced than the academies which Belva had attended. The name *seminary* didn't refer to a religious school, as it does today. It meant a private school, usually for young women.

It was a difficult time for Belva's family. On May 15, 1854, Cyrene died of a fever. The whole family was immensely saddened. Now Belva, the mother of a young child, was preparing to go off to the seminary. Most of Belva's family and friends disapproved of this move. They thought higher education was for men only—and certainly not for young mothers.

There was much to be done before she could go away to school. In order to finance her education, Belva had to sell the property in Gasport. With the help of her father-in-law, the sale was made and all debts paid. There was barely enough money left for tuition and living expenses in Lima, but Belva knew she could manage if she was very careful. She wouldn't be able to afford many trips home to see her daughter, for the seminary was sixty miles away.

In September 1854, Belva entered Genesee Wesleyan. Although her family and friends had thought Belva was going too far with her education, she soon decided she wasn't going far enough. She went to see President Cummings of nearby Genesee College (later Syracuse University) and told him she wanted to transfer from the seminary to the college.

President Cummings tried to discourage Belva. He told her other women had attended the college, but many lacked adequate preparation and found the courses too difficult. Belva insisted she could do the work in the four-year course. President Cummings finally agreed to let her enroll at Genesee College for the following term, right after Christmas vacation.

Belva was eager to make the change, but she was glad to have free time before she began. She was anxious to see her daughter.

It was good to be back home in Royalton with her family. Lura had grown so much! Belva must have spent many hours with Lura on her lap, telling her daughter and mother all the ideas she was hearing about.

There was a new book, *Uncle Tom's Cabin*, by Harriet Beecher Stowe. Everyone was reading it and talking about it, for it painted vivid pictures of the horrors of slavery. Another topic of discussion was the great number of people who were immigrating to the United States from Ireland and Germany. Many Americans thought these immigrants were too poor and dependent and should not be allowed in the country.

Another issue was women's rights. Six years earlier, the first women's rights convention had met in Seneca Falls, New York. To the shock and amusement of many Americans, the women issued their own Declaration of Independence. They demanded equal rights in education, jobs, suffrage (voting), and the ownership of property. These women were tired of being told all the things they couldn't do. They were working hard to change laws and opinions.

When she started Genesee College, Belva was working for women's rights in her own way. She was proving that a woman could learn as well as a man. College life wasn't easy. Breakfast was at 7:00 sharp, and no talking was allowed at the table. After that, there were four hours of recitation. Belva took "modern" subjects such as mathematics, magnetism, electrochemistry, political economy, and the Constitution of the United States. The students were required to study all afternoon and evening. The only recreation permitted was a walk after the evening meal. Like the other students, Belva supplied her "own lights, pails, wash-bowls, towels, and mirrors."

At the end of her first term, Belva learned that she could graduate in only two more years. She could do it by going to summer school before her senior year and by taking extra courses during the regular terms. This news came at a time when she didn't see how her money would stretch over three more years to graduation. Now it seemed possible to complete her education.

She went home to Royalton, full of her renewed hopes. They were dashed when her mother told her that she, too, had news. The Bennetts were moving to Illinois. They offered to take Lura with them.

How could Belva bear to be so far away from her daughter? The answer was simple: she must. The two of them spent the summer in Royalton with the Bennetts, and then they said good-bye. Mother and daughter wouldn't see each other for two years. Belva wouldn't be able to afford to visit, even at Christmas. Six-year-old Lura didn't fully understand why education was so important, but Belva did. She knew education was the key to a better life for herself and her daughter. As she had always done in the past, Belva looked toward her goal with single-minded determination. She returned to her studies.

In addition to her heavy schedule at the college, Belva made time to attend lectures given by a young lawyer in town. Because college officials thought a woman's attendance at such lectures was unladylike, they were displeased. But they could not forbid her as long as she did all her work at school. And Belva had had experience in going against tradition.

On one occasion, she actually slipped away from the college without the knowledge of the faculty. She went to a lecture by Susan B. Anthony, the famous women's rights leader. Dressed somberly in Quaker gray, Susan spoke forcefully of the need for women to work together to obtain property rights and the right to vote.

Finally, it was June 1857—a happy time. Belva would receive a bachelor of science degree, graduating with honors, and soon she could be with Lura again.

Then she received some news which should have been pleasant. She was offered the position of principal of the Lockport, New York, Union School District. This system joined all the schools in its region so that a high level of excellence could be achieved. The job sounded exciting, but it was to begin immediately after graduation. What about Lura? Now Belva wouldn't have time to go to Illinois. And even if she had time, she only had enough money for a one-way trip. So once again she made a very difficult decision. She decided to take the job and stay in Lockport until she could earn enough money to bring her daughter to live there. Then they could be together permanently, and Lura could attend school in the advanced Lockport system.

Only a few more months! she must have thought. She moved to Lockport, where she taught classes in higher mathematics, logic, rhetoric, and botany in addition to being principal. Belva was in charge of both teachers and students. Yet the men teachers earned $600 a year while their woman principal earned only $400!

The $400 salary was paid in three parts. By Christmas vacation, Belva had earned $133.33, enough money to make the trip to Illinois and bring Lura back. They had drawn pictures and written letters to each other for over two years, but now they could see a smile, hear a laugh, feel a kiss.

Warren and sixteen-year-old Inverno came to live with Belva and Lura. Inverno and Lura enrolled in Belva's school while Warren, a graduate engineer, took a job on the Lockport section of the Erie Canal. Once Belva had her brother, sister, and daughter settled, she could give full attention to her job.

Belva must have been a good administrator. In later years, she said jokingly of her days in Lockport that she had "six hundred boys and gals under one roof in one room without damage to either."

The new principal was determined to make changes in the way girls were taught. Girls didn't learn how to speak before an audience, and they weren't allowed to participate in sports. Belva thought this was nonsense. So did Susan B. Anthony. They served together on a New York School Association committee that decided it was beneficial for girls to learn public speaking. Immediately, Belva made public speaking one of the classes for her girls at Lockport. She also introduced her young women to gymnastics and took them on nature walks. And she convinced the school board members to support these changes.

Despite financial difficulties and the disapproval of others, Belva had gained a college degree. Now she was finding that she could help others attain a broader education.

Some little hills were being moved.

4 Some Big Changes

In 1861, after four years at Lockport, Belva decided to seek new opportunities. She accepted a job as principal of the Female Seminary in Gainesville, New York. But during the summer vacation, before Belva could begin her new job, a fire burned the Gainesville school. All the books and equipment and even students' clothing were destroyed. For one year, the school continued in temporary quarters with Belva as principal.

The new position was difficult and frustrating. Not only did Belva have to run the school from temporary quarters; she also had to deal with school officials who would have nothing to do with her advanced ideas. They were shocked when Belva suggested that the girls should learn to ice-skate in order to get exercise.

Perhaps the problems at Gainesville led Belva, one year later, to take charge of a new young ladies' seminary in neighboring Hornellsville. Then, in 1863, she learned that a young ladies' seminary in Owego, New York, was up for sale. She decided to buy the school.

If Belva had been married, the law wouldn't have allowed her to do this. Married women couldn't own property in their own name. But Belva was a widow, and there was no law to stop her, as long as she had the money. And she did.

When Belva was a student, she had lived frugally, scraping by because she had little. She must have continued to be thrifty, for in the six years after she graduated from college, she was able to build up savings.

Belva, who had struggled to put herself through Girls' Academy, Gasport Academy, and Genesee College, now bought the school in Owego and set about running it to suit herself.

Again, she introduced girls to higher mathematics, gymnastics, public speaking, and nature study. There must also have been discussion of the important questions of the day—women's rights, prohibition (banning the manufacture and sale of liquor), and abolition (the outlawing of slavery). All of these issues were connected in the minds of women who were interested in equality. They wanted the opportunity to vote, become educated, and hold property. They advocated prohibition because many women were mistreated and left in poverty as a result of their husbands' drinking. (The prohibition movement was also known as the temperance movement.) Many women were abolitionists, too, for their concern extended to others. They believed that slaves should be freed.

While Belva's students at Owego Female Seminary were discussing the slavery question, the Civil War was raging. Although she hated slavery, Belva was also a strong pacifist (a person who opposes war). She was against this war, just as she was against all others, for she believed there were peaceful ways to settle differences or right injustices.

Yet, once the war began, she believed everyone should participate in the struggle. She had taken a vacation trip around upstate New York in July 1862. In Elmira, New York, she saw some of the sick and wounded soldiers on their way home. She wrote that they "looked as though they had seen hard service, but were cheerful and hopeful." Belva was dismayed that some civilians were selfishly hoarding groceries and other goods because they feared the war would cause shortages. She noted the need for everyone to make sacrifices. "The burden of war is for all to bear," she wrote.

She had already followed her own advice. In the early months of the war, she had organized the Lockport students to knit wool shirts and knapsacks and to make sewing kits called "housewifes" (pronounced "husifs") for the Union soldiers of the Twenty-eighth Regiment.

When peace came in 1865, and the slaves were freed, Belva hadn't changed her mind about war. She looked at the cost in blood and treasure. She said that if the money spent, "including the amount paid and to be paid for pensions," was added up, there would have been enough "to have bought up every slave owned by the South six times over."

Belva had strong beliefs about almost all the issues of the day. She must have felt confined in the little towns of New York. A person with her energy and talents would want to be at the center of the action, the place where decisions were made. For Belva, that place was Washington, the District of Columbia.

The District of Columbia, usually abbreviated as D.C., isn't in any state. In 1791, Virginia and Maryland gave up some of their territory—sixty-nine square miles altogether—to create a federal district which would serve as the capital of the United States. When Belva moved there, the District's mayor and city council were elected by white male citizens. Women and black men who lived there couldn't vote at all. At that time, no one who lived in the District of Columbia could vote in national elections.

The District was the seat of government, and it was an exciting place to Belva. In her words, the nation's capital was a "great political centre—this seething pot." Here, she hoped to "learn something of the practical workings of the machinery of government, and see what the great men and women of the country felt and thought."

In February 1866, Belva sold Owego Female Seminary for nearly twice what she had paid for it and took herself and seventeen-year-old Lura to Washington, D.C. Soon they were seeing for the first time the buildings they had read about—the White House, the U.S. Supreme Court, and the Capitol, where members of Congress meet to make laws.

Before long, Belva was inside those buildings. During the afternoons, she observed sessions of Congress and the Supreme Court. She taught during the mornings at Harrover's Boarding and Day Academy, where part of her pay was tuition for Lura.

Belva wanted to go beyond the classroom. She went to meetings about women's rights, peace, and temperance. She read international law and the consular manual, and applied for the position of United States consul in Ghent, a river port in Belgium. (A U.S. consul is a person appointed to go to another country to represent U.S. interests and aid U.S. citizens who come there.) Belva's application was ignored. She was disappointed, but, in her words, she "was too weak-kneed to renew it." This disappointment didn't keep her from studying. She read more international law, and she studied Spanish and German.

In 1867, she decided to purchase property once again. By now Belva had supported herself and her daughter for ten years, had bought and sold a school, and was about to buy—of all things—meeting rooms. She purchased the Union League Hall on Ninth Street. She rented its large rooms (called halls) to political, religious, and temperance organizations. On the third floor of Union League Hall, mother and daughter had their living quarters.

Belva used rooms at Union League Hall for her new school, in which Lura taught the French and Latin classes. Belva called her school McNall's Academy. During the first year, it accepted girls only. But the program opened to boys in 1868. It was one of the first successful private schools in Washington which accepted both girls and boys.

From her first days in Washington, Belva had been part of the temperance, peace, and women's movements. Now that she owned the halls where meetings were held, she was even more involved. Offering facilities was not her most important contribution, however.

In 1867, the same year Belva bought Union League Hall, James and Julia Holmes established the Universal Franchise Association. They held their meetings in the hall. Belva became vice-president of the association, which was dedicated to bringing the vote (the franchise) to everyone—male or female, black or white.

Belva and her friends felt hopeful, for there were signs that opinions were changing. In England that year, a woman named Lily Maxwell had voted.

And her ballot was accepted. The event was reported in many newspapers. By the end of 1868, Representative George W. Julian had submitted to Congress the first proposal that all citizens, regardless of race or sex, should have the right to vote.

Ordinary citizens as well as congressmen had to be persuaded. Belva spoke at meetings both in the District and outside it, and not only at those events sponsored by the Universal Franchise Association. But she didn't dress as Julia Holmes did. Julia was called a bloomer girl because she wore bloomers— loose, flowing pants which were gathered at the ankle and worn under a "short" skirt (one which ended below the knees). As was the custom for women, Belva wore long skirts which swept the floor, and she often wore flowers in her hair. She wasn't trying to change the way women dressed. But she tried very hard to change the way they were seen.

At the women's rights meetings, people came to jeer and heckle the speakers. Sometimes the hecklers rolled vegetables or sent tin dishes clanking down the aisle. Newspapers often ridiculed what was said at the meetings. But the speakers encouraged each other, and most of those who came to listen helped, too. Among those who came to listen and to help was a dentist named Ezekiel Lockwood.

Dr. Lockwood was one of the first dentists to use nitrous oxide gas for "painless" tooth extraction. He advertised that he would "perform all dental operations at reduced prices." He was also a Baptist minister and had served as a chaplain during the Civil War. Afterward, he tried to help his men with their claims against the government. (When a person believes the United States government owes him money for some reason, he may decide to file a claim. Some of Dr. Lockwood's men sought pensions or back pay for military service. He helped them gather documents such as medical records and discharge papers to prove they had been in the army.) Tall and thin, Ezekiel Lockwood was a spry sixty-five-year-old. He was attracted to thirty-seven-year-old Belva.

In spite of the great difference in their ages, Belva was attracted to Ezekiel, too. They fell in love, and as Belva wrote jokingly years later, she "committed the indiscretion so common to the women of this country." She married

Ezekiel. The ceremony was in Union League Hall on March 11, 1868.

When Ezekiel moved into the apartment in Union League Hall, he moved his office there, too. Lura moved into a nearby boardinghouse but continued to teach at McNall's Academy. She was given increasing responsibilities there, so that she was soon running the school. Later that year, she married DeForest Ormes, a young man who had courted her before her mother had met Ezekiel. The young couple moved in with the Lockwoods.

On January 28, 1869, a daughter was born to Belva and Ezekiel. They named her Jessie Belva. Caring for a baby didn't prevent Belva from working for causes in which she believed. Perhaps having another daughter made her even more determined.

In the same year that Jessie was born, Belva and Ezekiel organized a Washington chapter of the Equal Rights Association. Shortly afterward, the association split in two. Some members began the American Woman Suffrage Association. Others, led by Elizabeth Cady Stanton and Susan B. Anthony, formed the National Woman Suffrage Association. This group was the one the Lockwoods chose. Its main goal was an amendment to the U.S. Constitution giving women the vote.

Belva was busy in the cause for women's rights. In those days, married women could not own property. They could not even inherit it. Their husbands controlled their property. Widows and women who had been deserted or who had alcoholic husbands were often penniless. There were few professions they could follow, for most of the doors to higher education were closed. The jobs that were available to women paid very little. Mothers didn't have the right to custody of their children in case of divorce.

Belva believed these injustices would cease if women had the vote. If women helped choose the lawmakers, surely the laws would change to bring equality in every area. She presented proposals to Congress, circulated petitions, gave speeches, and attended women's rights conventions. And once again she considered doing something that was unusual for a woman. She decided to go to law school.

5 *"The Real Fight of My Life"*

In the fall of 1869, when a law class opened at nearby Columbian College, Ezekiel and Belva were invited to attend the first lecture. It was presented by Dr. George W. Samson, president of the college. Belva also attended the second lecture. When she appeared at the third lecture and tried to pay the fee to join the class, her money was refused. She was told that the faculty would have to consider her application.

After two weeks she received this letter:

> Columbian College
> Oct. 7, 1869
>
> Mrs. Belva A. Lockwood:
> Madam—The Faculty of Columbian College have considered your request to be admitted to the Law Department of this institution, and, after due consultation, have considered that such admission would not be expedient, as it would be likely to distract the attention of the young men.
>
> Respectfully,
> Geo. W. Samson, President

This was a disappointment, but Belva wasn't going to let it stop her. She vowed to continue her efforts to study law.

The following year, something happened which seemed especially cruel. Eighteen-month-old Jessie became sick with typhoid fever. She died a few days later, on July 28, 1870.

This was one of the saddest times of Belva's life. Ezekiel, Lura, and the rest of the family mourned, too, and all of them comforted each other. In addition, Belva did what she had always done in times of grief—she turned to her work. No matter what happened, Belva always kept going.

A few months after Jessie's death, National University in Washington, D.C., opened a law school. When National's chancellor, William B. Wedgewood, agreed to teach law classes to women, Belva and fourteen other women signed up for the two-year program. Their work was to be the same as the men's. The women recited separately in their own classes, but they were allowed to attend the regular lectures.

Some of the young men began to grumble about having women in the lecture hall, and the school administrators began to back down. By the time Belva was ready for her last quarter, Chancellor Wedgewood informed his female students that they would no longer be allowed in the lecture rooms. But he promised to continue their separate classes so that they could finish the course of study. By then thirteen women had dropped out of the difficult program. Just Belva and Lydia S. Hall remained. Together they attended Mr. Wedgewood's classes.

In May 1872, Belva and Lydia passed the final exams. But they were to be denied the honor they had earned. Only the men received diplomas. The women weren't even permitted to share the graduation platform with the men. These men didn't want anyone to know that women could do what they had done.

Lydia got married and left the city, but Belva continued to fight for the right to practice law. She would later call this time "the real fight of my life."

Belva knew that a year earlier, the Supreme Court of the District of Columbia had struck the word "male" from its admission rules. And in February 1872, a black woman named Charlotte E. Ray had been granted a law diploma from Washington's Howard University. A Washington newspaper reported that she was "the first colored lady in the world to graduate in law." By April, Miss Ray had been admitted to the bar (permitted to practice law) in the District of Columbia. In May she was admitted to the bar of the Supreme Court of the District of Columbia.

Being a woman, then, was no longer a barrier to practicing law in the District. The biggest problem was that, unlike Charlotte Ray, Belva didn't have a diploma. But because of her work at National, she was certain she had the knowledge to be an effective lawyer.

There *was* a way to be admitted to the bar of a specific court without having a diploma. Belva would have to be introduced to that court by a member of its bar and then be examined on the points of law which were necessary for practicing there.

She asked a friend, Francis Miller, to move that she be admitted to the bar of the Supreme Court of the District of Columbia. Mr. Miller made the motion in July 1872. Belva waited to learn the dates for her examination. She heard nothing. So she went to the examination committee and demanded a hearing. The men didn't want to meet with her, but finally they agreed to do so. For three days, she answered their difficult questions.

After weeks of waiting to receive their report, she complained to Supreme Court Justice David K. Cartter. He appointed another committee. These men also questioned Belva for three days, and they, too, refused to report. They didn't like the idea of admitting women to the bar. Because Belva had no diploma, they could keep her out by failing to report her test results.

While struggling to gain admission to law school and to practice law, Belva hadn't forgotten the other injustices women suffered. At that time, the federal government employed several thousand women. Although some held positions of greater responsibility than men, no woman government employee could earn more than $75 a month. There was no such restriction for men. In 1870, Belva wrote a bill which she then helped to get through Congress. Called the Arnell bill after Congressman Arnell of Tennessee, who introduced it, it gave women government employees equal pay with men.

In 1871 she and seventy other women, including classmate Lydia S. Hall, had marched together to try to register to vote in the District. Although the election inspectors turned them down, the women went to the polls to vote, anyway. They were refused again. Outraged, the women brought suit in Justice Cartter's Supreme Court against the city election inspectors. They claimed that since they were citizens, they automatically had the right to vote.

The court's opinion, announced by Justice Cartter, was against them. It was clear that women were the only American citizens denied the right to vote, except for men who were criminals, mentally retarded, or insane. In March 1870, Congress had passed the Fifteenth Amendment to the Constitution. It said the right to vote could not be denied "on account of race, color, or previous condition of servitude." That meant that all black *men*, including former slaves, had the right to vote. Women—black or white—still could not! The men who passed the laws and the judges who interpreted them had again left women out. The members of the National Woman Suffrage Association were more certain than ever that a Constitutional amendment was necessary.

During the 1872 presidential election, Belva supported her friend Susan B. Anthony and fourteen other women when they actually cast ballots in Rochester, New York. The women were arrested and fined, and the inspectors who accepted their ballots were also arrested. But Susan wasn't about to quit, and neither was Belva. After the election, she tried new ways to become a practicing lawyer.

She decided to attend another law school. A new course of lectures was beginning at Georgetown University in Washington, D.C., so she went there. But the school refused to take her money. A few days later, a letter from the chancellor informed her that she couldn't become a member of the class.

Belva next tried Howard University. This was in 1873, a year after Charlotte E. Ray had graduated from the law school there. At least, Belva must have thought, her work at Howard would not be in vain, as it had been at National University. For a while Belva attended lectures at Howard. But soon she became overwhelmed with the unfairness of having to earn one degree twice. She was attending school to obtain a law degree. But she had already earned one! Belva decided that "the fight was getting monotonous and decidedly one-sided." Something different had to be done.

Since July 1872, Belva had actually been allowed to practice law in some places. Some of the justices of the peace in the District and Judge William B. Snell of the Police Court had told her that she would be recognized in their courts. Also, a Judge Olin had recognized her in the Probate Court of the District. (A probate court is one in which decisions about wills are made.) She had even brought suit over a contract in a court of one justice of the peace. The news of a woman lawyer's bringing suit was so astounding that it was telegraphed all over the country by the Associated Press!

Admission to a few lower courts did not satisfy Belva's desire to practice law. She needed that diploma. In her words, she "grew a little bolder, and to a certain extent desperate." In the fall of 1873, she wrote a short and daring letter. It was addressed to United States President Ulysses S. Grant, who was also ex officio president of the National University Law School.

This is what she wrote:

> No. 432 Ninth Street, N.W.
> Washington, D.C., September 3, 1873
> To His Excellency U. S. Grant, President, U.S.A.
> Sir: You are, or you are not, President of the National University Law School. If you are its President, I desire to say to you that I have passed through the curriculum of study in this school, and am entitled to, and demand, my diploma. If you are not its President, then I ask that you take your name from its papers, and not hold out to the world to be what you are not.
> Very respectfully,
> Belva A. Lockwood

Belva never received a reply from the president, but the next week the chancellor of the university gave her a diploma signed by the faculty and President Grant! Sixteen months had passed since she had earned her law degree. A few days later, she was admitted to the District bar, and then to the bar of the Supreme Court of the District.

At the age of forty-three, Belva was beginning a new career. Even today it takes a great deal of courage for a person to train for and enter a new profession at that age. And in those days, people couldn't expect to live as long as they do today. Belva's optimism, self-confidence, and determination were remarkable.

On her admission to the bar, the clerk of the District Supreme Court remarked, "You went through today, Mrs. Lockwood, like a knife. You see the world moves in our day."

Justice Cartter said, "Madam, if you come into this court, we shall treat you like a man." Justice Arthur McArthur told her: "Bring on as many women lawyers as you choose. I do not believe they will be a success."

Belva never worried about what people said, and she knew she would be a success. In the law office which she opened in her home, she had her hands full. Clients had been waiting for her to be admitted to fuller practice. Most of these clients were women.

Belva was very well known in Washington. She was five feet, six inches tall and had dark brown hair and black eyes. She wore black velvet dresses with white ruffles at the neck and wrists. When she went out, she wore black kid gloves and a blue cloth coat buttoned at the waist. She wore many kinds of beads and pins, and sometimes she wore a gold pendant in the form of a pair of scissors and a thimble. One of her favorite brooches showed the mythical god Mars driving a horse-drawn chariot.

When she entered the courtroom with her first case after her admission to the bar, people weren't curious about how she looked. They already knew that. They wanted to know how she would argue before the court.

Belva's first client was Mary Ann Folker, the mother of two children. She wanted a divorce. Her husband was a drunkard who beat her and did not give her enough money to feed the children. On September 29, 1873, Belva filed divorce papers for the case of *Folker* v. *Folker*.

Belva called neighbors who testified that Mr. Folker beat his wife. They also said that they had often seen him drunk, and that he had neglected the children. In addition to granting the divorce, the judge ordered Mr. Folker to pay attorney's fees and alimony to support his wife. But the judge told Belva that he didn't think Mr. Folker would ever pay, and that there was no law to make him do so. Belva, however, believed there was a way.

In 1873, people could be sent to jail if they failed to pay their debts. When Mr. Folker refused to pay alimony to Mrs. Folker, Belva took the case to court again, this time as a debt collection. She obtained a court order demanding payment. Mr. Folker still refused, so Belva had him sent to prison. Soon he decided that he'd rather pay alimony.

One of Belva's best-known cases was her defense of a woman accused of shooting a policeman. Looking for evidence, he had forced his way into her home. The woman admitted on the witness stand that she had fired the gun, and people thought that Belva had lost the case. But she was able to make use of a law which she personally didn't like and, in fact, had advocated changing.

She pointed out to the judge and jury that the District of Columbia was under the common law. Under that law, a woman must obey her husband without question. Belva's client had been told by her husband to shoot any man who tried to force his way into the house. When she shot the policeman, she was merely obeying her husband and, therefore, the law. The jury returned a verdict of "Not Guilty."

Belva's law practice grew. She asked her daughter to manage her office. McNall's Academy had been sold, along with the meeting rooms, but Lura had kept busy. Although she now had two daughters, she worked hard for women's rights and also wrote a weekly Washington newsletter for the *Lockport Daily Journal* under her maiden name, Lura McNall. But she made time to work with her mother again. While Lura and Belva were busy with clients, some of the young men who'd refused to be seen graduating with women were waiting for cases.

Belva's problem was different from the one those young men had. She had plenty of cases, but because she was a woman, she was barred from some courtrooms.

6 Going to the Supreme Court

The District Supreme Court is the highest court for the District of Columbia, but the U.S. Supreme Court and other United States, or federal, courts are also located in Washington, D.C. One of these federal courts is the U.S. Court of Claims.

In April 1874, Belva had an important case to argue before the U.S. Court of Claims. This is the court to which all claims against the government must be brought. Although Belva was a member of the District bar, she had not been admitted to practice in any federal courts. Before she could plead in the U.S. Court of Claims, she had to be accepted by the judges who presided there. She was nominated by A. A. Hosmer, a highly respected member of that court's bar. The five dignified justices listened to the nomination. There was a long pause, and everyone in the courtroom stared at the woman lawyer.

"Mistress Lockwood, you are a woman," Justice Drake said.

Belva joked later, "I began to realize that it was a crime to be a woman; but it was too late to put in a denial, and I at once pleaded guilty to the charge of the court."

The chief justice, Charles C. Nott, announced that the case would be put off until the next week.

The following week, Belva marched into the courtroom again, this time with her husband and some friends. When her case came before the justices, she stood up.

Susan B. Anthony (1820–1906), the suffragette leader.

When Belva gave her public lectures, they were announced by broadsides like this.

Lura McNall Ormes (1849–1894), Belva's daughter and co-worker.

Smithsonian Institution Photo No. 76-2569. Division of Political History.

THE NEGLECTED SIDE SHOWS—NOBODY SEEMS TO KNOW, THAT THEY ARE IN EXISTENCE.

Old Ben (*out of a job*).—"This ain't the year for side shows. The big circuses cover all the ground."

This cartoon from the 1884 election shows Belva, Benjamin Butler (wearing the letter "B"), and John P. St. John as a circus sideshow that nobody comes to watch. Instead, the crowd goes to see the Republican and Democratic candidates.

Smithsonian Institution Photo No. 78-16868. Division of Political History.

The Lockwood/Stow ballot in the 1884 presidential election.

Courtesy of Norma Wollenberg.

One hundred and two years after Belva's first campaign, the U.S. Postal Service issued a stamp in her honor.

BELVA LOCKWOOD,
THE EMINENT BARRISTER,
OF WASHINGTON, D. C.,

Who represented the Universal Peace Union at the Paris Exposition, and was their delegate to the International Congress of Peace in that city in 1889, and who was again elected and served as the delegate of the Peace Union to the International Peace Congress in London in 1890—making effective addresses in both congresses, one on "Arbitration" and the other on "Disarmament"—and who is one of the delegates of the Peace Union to the Congress in Rome the present season, is now prepared to favor Churches, Colleges, Teachers' Institutes, and Lecture Committees with any one of the following lectures, viz:

1. **The Paris Exposition and Social Life in Paris and London.**
2. **Is Marriage a Failure? No, Sir!**
3. **Women in the Professions.**
4. **Social and Political Life in Washington.**
5. **Across the American Continent.**
6. **The Tendency of Parties and of Governments.**
7. **The Conservative Force of the College and University with Practical Thoughts on University Extension.**

Belva gave speeches on many subjects, as this 1891 broadside shows.

Alfred Henry Love (1830–1913) founded the Universal Peace Union.

Belva Lockwood, date unknown.

This portrait of Belva wearing legal robes was painted by Nellie M. Horne in 1913. It hangs in the National Portrait Gallery, Washington, D.C.

"Mistress Lockwood, you are a married woman!" the chief justice declared.

That accusing declaration startled Belva. She took a deep breath, waved her hand toward her husband, and said, "Yes, may it please the court, but I am here with the consent of my husband." At these words, Dr. Lockwood stood and bowed to the court.

Nevertheless, the chief justice announced that the case would be put off for another week.

The judges met again, but they would not admit her. Belva had many clients and was building a strong reputation as a successful lawyer, but if a case had to be argued in the Court of Claims, she was forced to hand it over to a man. One male lawyer she had to hire did a poor job and lost Belva's case.

At once, she appealed the case to the U.S. Supreme Court. Carefully, she read the rule for admission to practice before this court. "Any attorney in good standing before the highest court of any State or Territory for the space of three years shall be admitted to this court when presented by a member of this bar." The rule said "attorney," not "man" or "male citizen." And Belva had been practicing before the highest court of the District since 1873. She hoped that by the time her case on appeal came up in the U.S. Supreme Court, she would have practiced for three years in the District of Columbia Supreme Court and would thus be eligible to appear before the U.S. Supreme Court. If she were admitted into the highest court in the country, she reasoned, other federal courts, such as the U.S. Court of Claims, could not keep her out.

Belva's experiences at the Court of Claims strengthened the desire for equality awakened years ago in Royalton, when she was offered half a man's salary. While she waited for her case to come before the nation's highest court, she continued to argue her cases in the District and work for women's rights.

The suffragettes (women fighting for their right to vote) began to plan a special event for the Centennial celebration of July 4, 1876, and Belva wanted to be part of it. The women were angry. One hundred years after the Declaration of Independence, they were still denied the right to vote and other rights of full citizenship because of their sex.

Ezekiel's health had been failing steadily for several years, and he was ill that July. But he shared Belva's concern for women's rights, and he knew the importance of the planned demonstration. He must have insisted she go.

Belva and the other women went to Philadelphia for the Independence Day celebration there. On the platform at Independence Hall was Thomas W. Ferry, acting vice president of the United States and a grandson of one of the signers of the Declaration of Independence. Immediately after an official read the familiar words of the 1776 declaration, Susan B. Anthony made her way to the front of the platform. She placed a document in the astonished Mr. Ferry's hand, saying that she was presenting him with a Declaration of Rights from the women citizens of the United States.

The women scattered copies of the document throughout the crowd and then left for their own rally. In front of an enthusiastic audience, Susan read from her copy of the women's document. She ended with these words: "We ask equality. We ask justice. We ask that all civil and political rights that belong to citizens of the United States belong to us and our daughters forever."

When Belva returned to Washington after the celebration, she continued her quest for admission to the U.S. Supreme Court and the U.S. Court of Claims. In October 1876, after she had practiced before the District Supreme Court for three years, a lawyer named A. G. Riddle introduced her to the United States Supreme Court. The nine judges looked at Belva in amazement. They put off their decision for a few days, but when Belva stood before them again, they didn't have good news.

The judges said that admitting women had no precedent, meaning that it hadn't been heard of before in English law.

When judges make decisions, they look for precedents in the law. They cannot make laws; they only interpret them. This nation is fairly young, so there have been cases for which there were no laws and no precedents. Because laws in the United States were patterned after England's, precedence was often sought in English law.

The Supreme Court judges told Belva that because they could see no

English precedence, there would have to be some other indication such as public opinion or a special law before they would admit her.

Belva couldn't believe her ears. No English precedent! What about Queen Elizabeth? She had ruled all of England and administered its laws from 1558 to 1603.

The next year, Belva was the main speaker at the convention of the National Woman Suffrage Association, founded by Susan B. Anthony and Elizabeth Cady Stanton. "I have been told that there is no precedent for admitting a woman to practice in the Supreme Court of the United States," she exclaimed to her audience. "The glory of each generation is to make its own precedents. As there was none for Eve in the Garden of Eden, so there need be none for her daughters on entering the colleges, the church, or the courts."

About that same time, Belva joined an organization formed by peace-loving citizens under the leadership of Alfred Love. Alfred was the son of a well-to-do Quaker family in Philadelphia. He had argued against the Civil War and had refused to fight. He had also refused to pay any taxes that would support the war or to handle army orders in his woolen textile business. Alfred lost the family business because he wouldn't compromise. In 1875, he organized the association called the Universal Peace Union.

The group's aim was to preserve peace through arbitration. They would, when asked by two warring parties, listen to both sides and find a resolution that was fair to all. Alfred's group had already helped settle some disputes between England and the United States. Belva had always been a pacifist, and peace was as important to her as equality. She was glad to be a member of this group.

Then, once again, tragedy struck. On April 23, 1877, Belva's beloved Ezekiel died. He had stood beside her, encouraged her, loved her. And now he was gone. At age forty-six, she had seen two husbands, a baby daughter, and a younger sister die. And while grief over Ezekiel's death was still fresh, her father died on June 26, 1877. It must have seemed at times too much to bear.

But Belva did bear it. Her family helped her. Lura, DeForest, and their two little girls were a comfort. Hannah Bennett, left alone when her husband died, came to live with her daughter, granddaughter, and great-granddaughters. And Belva corresponded with her sister Inverno and brother Warren, as she'd done over the years, keeping informed about her nieces and nephews and now, their children. (There is no record of correspondence with Rachel.)

In spite of her grief, Belva kept working. She still had a personal fight on her hands, the fight to be admitted to the U.S. Supreme Court. What was Belva to do? The justices had declared that there was no precedent for her admission to the court. How could she win public opinion supporting her admission? How could she get Congress to pass a law allowing her to practice before the Supreme Court?

In the fall of 1877, some newspaper men in Washington became interested in the long and unequal battle she'd been waging. They came to her office and asked her what she intended to do next.

"Get up a fight all along the line," she answered. "I shall ask again to be admitted to the bar of the Supreme Court; I shall myself draft a bill and ask its introduction into both houses of Congress."

They told her they would help.

With newspaper publicity and the gathering of public opinion on her side, senators and representatives began to back Belva's bill.

Over the previous two years, she had persuaded friends in Congress to introduce bills which would allow women lawyers to appear before the U.S. Supreme Court. In 1876, Congressman Benjamin F. Butler had drafted and introduced a bill for the admission of women to that bar. After debate, the bill lost. In 1877, a second bill was drafted by Congressman William G. Lawrence. According to Belva, it "died almost before it was born."

Now, in December 1877, Congressman John M. Glover introduced Belva's bill. It became known as H.R. 1077 (House of Representatives bill number 1077). Soon Belva was called before the House Committee on the Judiciary to defend it. The committee gave a favorable report, recommending the bill to the other members of the House. And the bill passed the House early in the session by a two-thirds majority.

Senator Aaron A. Sargent took charge of the bill in the Senate Judiciary Committee. Because there was no specific law stating that women could *not* practice before the Supreme Court, committee members decided there was no need for a law stating that they could! So in April 1878 they refused to recommend H.R. 1077 to the rest of the Senate. At the next session, in May, Mr. Sargent resubmitted the bill, and the committee again considered it. Still, the committee refused to recommend H.R. 1077. This time, Senator Sargent had the bill put on the calendar of the entire Senate for the following session, to be considered "on its own merits." This meant that the Senate would consider Belva's bill without a recommendation from the committee.

When Senator Sargent became ill and had to go to Florida, the issue was put off. Belva persuaded senators Joseph E. McDonald and George F. Hoar to help with the bill. But not until February 1879 was H.R. 1077 brought to the floor of the Senate. By this time, Senator Sargent had recovered, and he again took up the fight. He declared the issue "merely a measure of justice."

"In this land man has ceased to dominate over his fellow," Senator Sargent said, referring to the end of slavery and the granting of the vote to black men. "Let him cease to dominate over his sister."

Senator Hoar supported women's rights, but he showed another way of viewing the matter. He said that the bill wouldn't merely admit women to a professional privilege. It would allow every citizen—man or woman—to choose his or her own lawyer. Without H.R. 1077, if a man chose a woman lawyer and his case was taken to a different court, he often had to change to a man lawyer. Thus, men would also benefit from the bill.

The men who spoke for Belva's bill were persuasive, but she was afraid there wouldn't be enough votes. She knew she had to lobby. This is the practice of talking to lawmakers outside the voting chamber in an effort to influence their votes. In writing about her efforts later, she said, "Nothing was too daring for me to attempt. I addressed Senators as though they were old familiar friends, and with an earnestness that carried with it conviction."

On February 7, 1879, the Senate passed H.R. 1077 with 39 yeas, 20 nays, and 17 absent. Belva sent flowers to those who had helped her win.

President Rutherford B. Hayes signed the bill into law a few days later. The fight had lasted five years from the time she was first refused by the Court of Claims. In spite of setbacks along the way, Belva had never given up. In spite of the days when she must have felt tired and discouraged, Belva had been convinced that she would win—no matter how long it took.

Now the law was clear. Qualified women had the right to argue cases before the Supreme Court of the United States. To be qualified, a woman had to have a good record and have been a member of the bar of the highest court of any state or territory for three years. In Washington, D.C., this court was the Supreme Court of the District. Belva qualified.

She immediately applied to practice before the United States Supreme Court. She was the first woman admitted to its bar. Of more practical importance to her, however, was her acceptance to the U.S. Court of Claims. It followed soon after her admission to the Supreme Court. The struggle to admit women to the bar was won.

7 Another Mountain to Move

The years of struggle and her personal tragedies didn't wear Belva down. She maintained the vigor that she had had as a country girl riding bareback on a farm horse. She had shown a special liveliness to her female students when she taught them exercises. And sometimes she allowed the people of Washington to see a gleeful side of her energetic personality.

An item from the *Lockport Daily Union* on April 25, 1878, reported: "Mrs. Marilla M. Ricker, Mrs. Belva Lockwood and Mrs. Dundore, three female lawyers of Washington, engaged in a foot race in a suburban street in Washington last week, and Mrs. Lockwood won." There were no joggers in the 1870s. To an onlooker on that spring day, the sight of three women holding up their long skirts and petticoats as they raced must have seemed strange indeed. But the hard-working trio sometimes found time for lighthearted fun.

Belva found something else which expressed her vigorous, merry side as well as her practicality. It was a tricycle. The tall three-wheelers were becoming quite popular for men but were not considered ladylike. Instead, women, wearing the long skirts of the day, were supposed to walk as though they were floating—to "skim over the ground without appearing to use their legs," as one 1980s writer put it. As soon as Belva saw her first trike, however,

she decided that it would be her mode of transportation. She was always so busy she needed some simple way to get around the city quickly. Her trike had a special dashboard that kept her skirts down.

A few days after the president signed H.R. 1077 into law, Belva bought a twenty-room house on F Street, moving in with Lura, DeForest, their daughters, and Hannah. Belva invited Lavinia Dundore and Marilla Ricker, her competitors in the footrace reported in Lockport, to share office space with her in the F Street house.

Marilla was known as one who "fears neither God, man nor the devil, because she does not believe particularly in any of them." The three women became known as "the three graces," after three sister goddesses in Greek mythology. They hired Lillie Sadler as their typist (known then as a "typewriter"). There were other women lawyers in the District by this time, including Emma M. Gillett and Laura DeForce Gordon.

Belva's office had sturdy mahogany desks and chairs and portraits of George Washington, Martha Washington, and Abraham Lincoln on the walls. Her letterhead read:

BELVA A. LOCKWOOD, ATTORNEY AND SOLICITOR, 619 F STREET N. W.

Practice before the District Courts, United States
Supreme Court, and Court of Claims.
PENSION, BOUNTY AND LAND CLAIMS A
SPECIALTY.
PATENTS OBTAINED.

Belva would take any kind of case, but she specialized in claims of soldiers and sailors for back pay and pensions. In 1875, feeling that soldiers had usually received what was owed them while sailors were neglected, she had gotten a bill passed allotting $50,000 in special payments for sailors and marines. Any cause involving oppression or inconsistencies in the law was of particular interest to her. And she didn't forget her own recent struggle to win admission to the United States Supreme Court. One of her first acts before that bar was to sponsor Samuel R. Lowry for admission. He was the fourth black man, and the first from the South, to be admitted to practice there.

Lawyer Lockwood did more than work on clients' cases. She was a popular lecturer, she wrote articles for newspapers and journals, and she was active in arguing the cause of equal rights for women. She and her friends Susan B. Anthony and Elizabeth Cady Stanton worked tirelessly for women's rights. In New York state, Belva and Susan had fought together to change some school rules. Now they continued their struggle to obtain a Constitutional amendment allowing women to vote.

In 1880, at a meeting led by Susan, Belva quoted the Constitution. "We the people," she repeated, declaring that she'd never heard of a "people" made up of men alone. "There are 110,500,000 male voters in the United States," she remarked, "and 12,500,000 women property owners. Should they not have something to say about what is done with the taxes they pay? If the Constitution does not allow women to vote, then the Constitution should be amended or abolished!"

Republican women in Washington chose Belva to represent them at the Republican national convention in Chicago that year. Much of Chicago had burned in the great fire of 1871, and the city was still being rebuilt. The elegant Palmer House, where the convention was held, had just been completed. Hundreds of new buildings were rising in that city of almost 700,000 people. At every turn, delegates could see frames of iron girders, hinting at what the skyline soon would be. The iron trestles were part of a new technique which made very tall buildings possible.

At the Palmer House, almost four thousand delegates jammed into a convention hall meant for two thousand. The noisy, smoky hall was filled with men and very few women. Many ballots were taken, but no decision as to the Republican presidential candidate could be reached. There were private sessions, however, in which a choice was finally made. Belva, like most of the delegates, was not invited to these meetings. James Garfield, who later won the election, was the compromise nominee for president.

Once the nominee had been selected, the platform (the party's goals and policies) could be constructed. Belva stood before the platform committee to read the plank (a statement of purpose) which she had drafted. It was a resolution that the Republican party would pledge "to secure to women the exercise of their right to vote." The plank didn't pass the platform committee. The men didn't think it was important.

Four years later, in 1884, Belva and her friends again tried to get a commitment for woman suffrage into the platform at the Republican convention. Again, the men refused to consider it.

Another woman, Frances Willard, also tried to get a plank passed by the committee in 1884. She had come with a resolution on temperance. Miss Willard spoke to the committee and presented a petition signed by twenty thousand people. In the audience were distillers, men who made their living from the sale of alcoholic beverages. When the chairman asked what should be done with the temperance petition, some of the men shouted that it should be kicked under the table. With that, the petition was swept to the floor.

That gesture showed the lack of respect the men had for the women's concerns. Even after such treatment, Susan and Elizabeth urged members of the National Woman Suffrage Association to work within an established party and to vote for the Republican presidential nominee, James G. Blaine. Belva was outraged.

Angrily, she wrote a letter to Susan and sent copies to the editors of different newspapers.

"Why not nominate women for important places?" she asked in the letter. "Is not Victoria Empress of India?. . .If women in the States are not permitted to vote, there is no law against their being voted for. . . .We shall never have rights until we take them, nor respect until we command it."

One copy of the letter went to Marietta Stow of San Francisco, the editor of a newspaper called the *Woman's Herald of Industry*. Marietta answered Belva's letter. She wrote that Belva had been nominated for president by the Equal Rights party, a newly formed group in San Francisco.

It wasn't unusual for smaller parties to nominate candidates. In addition to the Republican, Blaine, and the Democratic candidate, Grover Cleveland, other men were running for president in 1884. Two of the most prominent were John P. St. John, Prohibition party, and Benjamin F. Butler, Greenback party.

Nevertheless, the nomination from the women in San Francisco astonished Belva. She stuck the letter in her pocket and kept it a secret for several days.

One day when Belva was at the District Supreme Court to file some papers, the assistant clerk of the court told her that she should throw her support to Benjamin Butler.

"Why should I do that?" she asked.

The clerk replied that Mr. Butler believed in woman suffrage, was a temperance man, and wanted to improve conditions for working people— all causes which Belva had supported.

She couldn't keep her secret any longer. "Clancy, I've got a nomination for myself," Belva confided.

The clerk laughed and answered, "That's the best joke of the season!"

Belva hurried from the courthouse, jumped on her wheels, and sped away to mail her acceptance of the nomination for president of the United States.

8 *Mother Hubbards March for Belva*

To Belva's dismay, Susan and Elizabeth didn't support her. They believed that a woman's candidacy at that time would do no good. They knew she couldn't possibly win, and they feared that her campaign would take the focus away from their struggle for women's rights. They had felt the sting of ridicule, and they believed that Belva's candidacy would bring even more of it.

Other critics accused her of running for president to get publicity for her law practice and lecture billings. Although the fears Susan and Elizabeth had about Belva's candidacy were well-founded, the charges about publicity were untrue. Belva didn't need additional publicity. She couldn't have been any busier.

In spite of the criticism, Belva had already accepted the nomination, and she knew there was no turning back.

"Now let us see what a few earnest, capable women can do," she had written in her acceptance letter. She urged the women of the Equal Rights party to hold a state convention in California. They did this, adding Marietta Stow's name to the ticket as the nominee for vice president.

Again, Belva came under attack from others, including Susan and Elizabeth. They objected because she and Marietta had only been nominated by a California, rather than a national, convention. And they believed Marietta was simply seeking publicity for herself and her unusual theories. Marietta designed her own clothes, consisting of a man's trousers under a kilt skirt. She put forth some strange ideas, such as belief in an electric shock treatment to cure all kinds of illnesses and the virtue of a diet of cold food only. But she worked hard for the Equal Rights party, and Belva knew her as a strong supporter of woman suffrage.

Belva wasn't the first woman to announce her *intention* to run for president. In 1872, Victoria Woodhull had announced she would run. Belva had made a speech in support of her candidacy in New York City. Then Miss Woodhull had discovered she wasn't old enough to run (she was not yet thirty-five), and her campaign had ended before it began. Belva was the first woman to run for president.

Belva felt that if her ticket could win the election in just one state, her campaign would "pass into the history of 1884, and become the entering wedge—the first practical movement in the history of Woman Suffrage."

The Equal Rights party didn't concern itself with women only. Mass education (free education for all), pensions for disabled soldiers, an increase in wages for working men and women, and the right of Indians to govern themselves were a few of the planks in its platform.

Drawn up by Belva from rough notes when she was besieged by reporters in her office, the platform began with this statement: "We pledge ourselves, if elected to power, to do equal and exact justice to every class of our citizens, without distinction of color, sex or nationality."

On a Maryland farm, a group of Washington women held a meeting to approve the nominations that had been made in California. There were speeches and a picnic, with pies, cakes, sandwiches, and lemonade set out on long tables under spreading apple trees. Many reporters were present, and Lura and Hannah were there, too. Writing about the meeting later, Belva remembered: "It grew dark before I rose to speak. I have a vivid recollection when my turn came of seeing nine reporters on railroad ties, trying to take down my words by the light of one flickering candle."

The candidate worked very hard. She made speeches, talked to reporters, and traveled widely. When people made fun of her, she just shrugged. All the candidates endured ridicule, but the jokes about Belva centered on the fact that she was a woman. It was reported that she dyed her hair black, that she had tried to bribe a judge with chocolate caramels, that she wore scarlet underwear while riding her tricycle, that she couldn't decide whether to endorse the new style of "split skirts," and that she was really a divorced woman originally named Tillie Wilkins.

This last charge was the only one to which Belva publicly replied. Writing to the editor of the *New York World*, she stated that her true name was Belva Ann Bennett McNall Lockwood, and that she had never been known by any other names. She wrote, "Both of my husbands were good men, kind and devoted husbands, lived honored and respected and died lamented, and I trust I shall never cast dishonor upon their memory."

Belva carried her message to Philadelphia, Chicago, and Cincinnati. She spoke at New York's Academy of Music and Cleveland's Opera House. Wearing a black velvet gown and a corsage of roses, she stepped on stage after stage to insist on equality for women.

"In this free Republic," she proclaimed, "contrary to the Bill of Rights, we are governed without our own consent."

It wasn't easy to campaign in those days. The only practical transportation was the railway. After spending long, weary hours on trains, candidates had to appear fresh and vigorous while making speeches.

And speaking at a political rally was difficult. After a parade through town—a torchlight parade if it was a night meeting—the milling crowd entered a large room. The people didn't take seats and quietly await the program. Instead, supporters marched, cheered, and sang songs while hecklers jeered and threw vegetables. Even after the speeches began, people pushed, shoved, and argued loudly. Sometimes disputes ended with the participants rolling on the dusty floor, pounding each other with their fists. Throughout, reporters shouted questions. After a long day of travel, a candidate had to shout above the din, ignore the thickening cloud of cigar smoke, and appear to enjoy the whole affair. The fact that big crowds came to cheer Belva in every city helped her keep going.

Criticism continued. One newspaper called Belva's candidacy "one of the sad features of the Presidential campaign." The article went on to state that the campaign was bringing contempt upon woman suffrage, and that the "damage done by her and a little band of eccentric zealots in San Francisco cannot be estimated."

Other newspapers reflected different views of Belva's candidacy. The *Buffalo Express* referred to her as a "Star-eyed Goddess of Reform," but the *Rochester Post Express* printed these words: "Belva Lockwood is asking the men to support her, the immodest minx!" The *Lockport Daily Union* published this poem:

My soul is tired of politics
Its vicious ways, its knavish tricks;
I will not vote for any man
But whoop it up for Belva Ann.

Even lighthearted support, such as the *Daily Union*'s poem, could be a little embarrassing. Another example of such doubtful assistance was the Mother Hubbard clubs. It was common at that time to have political clubs made up of young men who dressed in strange costumes and sought publicity for their candidates. The men who supported Belva wore "Mother Hubbards" (long, loose dresses) and "poke bonnets" (large hats with long bills). They sang and made speeches. There was always one person who pretended to be Belva, and he would make a campaign speech. These speeches were often covered in the newspapers as though Belva had really been there. The Mother Hubbard club members also went out into the streets with brooms, symbolizing "a clean sweep" with Belva. Although the candidate sometimes wondered whether the young men were really helping, she felt that they "actually did some creditable work" in Terre Haute, Indiana.

It was in Indiana that Belva and Marietta claimed victory. They didn't have the largest popular vote, but the electors of the state voted for them.

Americans don't vote directly for president and vice president. Instead, they cast their ballots for *electors*, who in turn vote for the candidates of their party. The number of a state's electors equals the number of its senators and representatives in Congress. The total number of voters who cast their ballots is called the *popular vote*. After the popular vote is counted, the chosen electors come together to vote. Electors are supposed to vote for the candidates of their party. Some states require it. But there is no federal law that says electors can't change their minds.

The winning electors in Indiana at first cast their votes for the Democratic candidate, Cleveland, who had won the popular vote in the national election. But then they decided to vote for Belva Lockwood. Although the electors had the right to switch their support, the United States Congress refused to accept the changed votes.

Belva petitioned the Senate and House of Representatives. In the petition, she listed her popular vote in six states and the electoral vote of Indiana:

New Hampshire . . . . 379 votes

New York . . . . 1336 votes

Michigan . . . . 374 votes

Illinois . . . . 1008 votes

Maryland . . . . 318 votes

California . . . . 734 votes

and the entire electoral vote of Indiana.

Belva demanded that the vote of Indiana be given to her. Congress refused.

The popular vote listed in Belva's petition totalled 4,149. The Equal Rights party also received half of the electoral vote of Oregon and a large popular vote in Pennsylvania. In those days, of course, there were no computers to count the votes. Counting was done by hand. Sometimes those in charge of counting threw away ballots for candidates they didn't like. Belva's Pennsylvania votes weren't counted. They were dumped into a wastebasket.

Thus ended the first presidential campaign by a woman in the United States. There had been criticism and mockery, popular votes had been thrown away in Pennsylvania, and electoral votes had gone unrecognized in Congress. But Belva didn't feel defeated. She believed that the effort had "awakened the women of the country" as nothing else had done. And men became more aware, too. After all, more than four thousand men had voted for a woman president! Cleveland and Blaine each received close to five million votes, so the vote for Belva was only a tiny portion of the total. But most of the men who supported Belva probably had never considered voting for a woman before her campaign. She hadn't failed.

9 *"Suffrage Is No Longer an Issue"*

In 1885, Belva presented to Congress a bill she had written. It asked for the establishment of an international court to preserve peace in the world. The members of Congress wouldn't take any action on her bill, but the State Department sent her to Europe in 1886 to attend the Congress of Charities and Corrections in Geneva, Switzerland. This was the first world peace conference.

Belva was asked to read her proposal at the conference. Some of the delegates requested copies so that they could present such bills in their countries. She came home to her law practice determined to do all she could to bring about world peace.

The following year Belva represented the United States at the Second International Peace Conference. This time it was held in Budapest, Hungary. From there, she went to London to attend the International Woman's Congress. She presented a paper titled "The Civil and Political Life of Women in the United States."

In 1888 the Equal Rights party once again nominated Belva Lockwood for president of the United States. This time the vice presidential candidate was Alfred H. Love, the man who had organized the Universal Peace Union.

It was felt that a party dedicated to equal rights should have a man as well as a woman on its ticket. The party distributed campaign buttons with the words "Love Our Lockwood" framing a picture of Belva.

Alfred Love was respected and admired by many people, even those who didn't agree with his policies. With him on the ticket, the public seemed more willing to see the candidates as dignified and sincere. There weren't any antics like those of the Mother Hubbard clubs in this campaign.

Belva worked just as hard this time as she had four years earlier. When she traveled, she carried a banner inscribed with the word "Peace" on one side and "Women's Rights" on the other. Neither the Democrats nor Republicans endorsed her ideas, but the run for the presidency gave her a big audience. Nevertheless, she didn't get as many votes on her second try as she had in 1884. A Republican, Benjamin Harrison, won the election.

After the second campaign, she spent more and more of her time giving lectures. People loved to hear her, and she always drew big crowds. Her topics covered just about everything, including government, banking, temperance, peace, and marriage. One popular lecture was titled "Is Marriage a Failure? No, Sir!"

A report in the *Brooklyn Daily Eagle* on July 27, 1888, called her talk "Tendencies of Parties and Governments" "an intellectual treat." The article went on to say that "brains are what Belva is troubled with."

It's easy to imagine how she looked as she gave her lectures. She believed fervently in what she was saying. She might have walked back and forth across the stage, the train of her long velvet dress sweeping the floor, perhaps stirring up little dust clouds. Her strong soprano voice would have rung throughout the hall.

Women's rights continued to be a common theme for her speeches. In one speech, she would ask questions of the audience. "Has God given one half of his creatures talents and gifts that are but as a mockery—wings but not to fly? Reasoning ability, but not to think, the power of poetry, but not to write? The power to sway the multitude with her eloquence but not to voice the thoughts?" She shouted the answer: "We tell you nay!"

In another of her speeches, she said, "I am a practical woman. If I can't get what I want, I take what I can get." Yet she once admitted to a reporter, "I am very simple minded. When I wish to do a thing, I only know one way—to keep at it till I get it."

While she was making speeches, she still maintained her law office. And she remained in the peace movement. She was a delegate to international peace conventions in 1889 in Paris, 1890 in London, 1891 in Rome, and 1892 in Berne, Switzerland. At the Paris meeting, she delivered a paper in French on international arbitration. She also made speeches about disarmament at the meetings.

Lura kept the office running smoothly during her mother's absences. She continued working even after she had a third child, in 1890. This time she had a son. He was named DeForest, after his father.

In 1891, an old client came to see Belva. He was Jim Taylor, a Cherokee Indian from North Carolina. Years before, she had won cases for him in the United States Court of Claims, and he had promised to introduce her to members of his tribe who needed help. He and Belva had signed a legal document agreeing to share the fees which Belva might earn in these cases. Now the tribe was asking Belva's help in collecting money owed by the United States government.

The claim had its beginnings in 1835 with the Treaty of New Echota. Then there had been almost sixteen thousand Cherokees in North Carolina, Tennessee, Alabama, and Georgia. Only seventy-nine Cherokees had signed the treaty, which transferred title of the land away from the Indians and exchanged their land for a new Indian territory in Oklahoma. In addition to getting the western territory, the Indians were supposed to be paid for their eastern land. But those few who signed the treaty didn't speak for most of the others. The majority hadn't wanted to move. They hadn't wanted the money. They wanted to remain where their tribe had always lived. Most of the Cherokees had refused to go west.

In 1838, U.S. troops forced the Indians to move to Oklahoma. Of the fourteen thousand who were marched through bitter winter weather, four thousand died. This journey has been called the "Trail of Tears." But some of the Indians never took that journey. More than a thousand Cherokees escaped from the soldiers and hid in the Great Smoky Mountains in North Carolina.

In 1891, the descendants of these North Carolina Cherokees obtained a treaty which allowed them to work their land legally. Now they wanted Belva to help them collect the money owed all the Indians from the original treaty of 1835. The government didn't dispute owing a million dollars, the purchase price of the land. The claim which Belva brought was for interest as well. The interest had built up so that it totaled more than the original million dollars.

Belva knew that this case would take years to prepare. She was defending three or four thousand families—twelve or fifteen thousand people. The claim money would have to be divided among them. She had to review all the documents written about the United States and the Cherokee nation. She had to travel to the Indian territories to interview claimants.

While Belva was doing her research or interviewing the claimants, Lura managed the office, and she kept the Cherokee case up to date when her mother was traveling on other business. Then tragedy struck again. In 1894, Lura suddenly died.

How could Belva go on without her daughter, her co-worker, her closest friend? She had the Cherokee claim and the causes of peace and women's rights to work for. But she felt a deep emptiness at this great loss. Her little grandson helped to fill that void. Belva volunteered to help care for young DeForest. Six years later, when DeForest was ten years old, his father died. Belva was left again with a child to support.

Tirelessly, Belva kept working. She didn't abandon the cause of women's rights. She joined with other women to draft a bill providing a fair inheritance law for married women. The bill also gave married women the right to sue, to buy and sell property, to enter into contracts, and to otherwise conduct business. Perhaps most important, the bill guaranteed the right of guardianship. It said that a man couldn't throw his wife out of the house and keep the children unless he could prove she was unfit as a mother. This bill was called the Married Woman's Property Act.

President William McKinley signed the bill into law on June 1, 1896. Belva presented an embossed copy of the new law to the women of the National American Woman Suffrage Association. (The National Woman Suffrage Association and American Woman Suffrage Association had merged in 1890.)

The case of the Eastern and Emigrant Cherokees against the United States was heard in the United States Court of Claims in 1905. The presiding judge was Charles C. Nott, who had opposed Belva's admission into this same court in 1874. "A woman is without legal capacity to take the office of attorney," he had said then. So in addition to Belva's desire that the Indians be compensated fairly, she felt a personal challenge.

She must have been pleased by the government attorney's opening remarks. "You have before you today in this court of large cases, the largest case that has ever been brought before it," he said. He asked the court not to be "biased about the talk of these poor Cherokees," because the "poor Cherokees" were very well represented. He referred to Belva as "the most noted woman attorney in this country if not in the world."

Judge Nott announced his decision on March 20, 1905. He declared that the United States had "broken and evaded the letter and spirit" of the Treaty of New Echota. However, he refused to allow the full interest claimed. Belva appealed the case to the United States Supreme Court.

When she was asked why she claimed interest when the government was willing to pay a million dollars, her answer was short: "Because it was an interest-bearing fund." On April 30, 1906, Chief Justice Fuller delivered the Supreme Court's decision: "We agree that the United States are liable. The monies should be paid directly to the equitable owners."

At age seventy-five, Belva had won nearly five million dollars for the Cherokee Indians! Almost four million was accumulated interest on the amount promised by the original treaty. Newspapers reported that she had won the largest private claim ever allowed against the government. Her share of the fees was about fifty thousand dollars.

This would have been a fitting time to close the office door and rest. But Belva wasn't ready to quit. In 1909 she received the honorary degree of doctor of laws from Syracuse University. She was the first woman in the United States to receive that title. And she continued to look for ways to advance the cause of women. Late in her life, she suggested to some friends that they form a feminine "army." Her plan was to take two hundred women to the Capitol and ask permission for two or three of them to speak to Congress about woman suffrage. Once this request was granted, all two hundred would enter and keep on talking. If the women didn't get permission, they'd just go in anyway. She couldn't get her friends to go along with her idea.

Belva continued to be active in the peace movement, too. She was a delegate to almost every international peace conference held between 1886 and 1911. Her law practice had slowed somewhat by 1911, when she was eighty-one, but even then she noted that she had "three heavy law cases on hand." That year she accepted an invitation to go for a plane ride in an exhibition sponsored by an airplane company. A newspaper article about her in 1912 noted that "one day last week she appeared for clients in three different courts of the city."

In 1914, a suffragist organization called the Congressional Union presented a resolution to Congress. The members demanded a Constitutional amendment giving women the right to vote. Belva, who was eighty-three years old, stood at the top of the Capitol steps to receive the five hundred delegates and to march in with them.

Belva had earned a great deal of money in her lifetime. From a young woman who had to stretch every dollar to get an education, she had become a financially comfortable lawyer. But in her old age she listened to bad investment advice. She lost her life's savings. Yet this wasn't a great tragedy for a woman who had endured so many disappointments. She still had her home and enough income to support herself.

Another blow fell in 1914. Her Cherokee friend Jim Taylor had died, and his heirs, in looking over his papers, had found the contract between him and Belva. In the Eastern and Emigrant Cherokee case, Jim hadn't received his share. Doubtless the two old friends had decided to forget the agreement in that case since Jim was a beneficiary of the court's decision. But his heirs wanted the money. The Indians won their case against Belva for nine thousand dollars.

She didn't have the money. A public appeal asking people to help her pay the Indians failed. Although she had helped many people over the years, the sum wasn't raised, and at age eighty-three, she had to sell her home to pay her debt.

That same year, she made her last trip to Europe. She was one of eighteen American women sent by the State Department to present a peace message to women throughout the world.

She argued her last case in court, the settlement of an estate, at the age of eighty-four. In 1916, she made her last public message, an endorsement of President Woodrow Wilson for reelection. The speech was printed and circulated as campaign material. Still believing that arbitration could end war, she hoped that Wilson would be able to organize a world League of Nations, where countries could resolve their quarrels peacefully.

Although the United States Congress never approved Wilson's League of Nations, the other cause to which Belva had given so much time was gaining ground. The Wyoming Territory had given women the vote in 1869 and the Utah Territory followed suit the next year. Woman suffrage was granted in Colorado in 1893 and in Idaho in 1896. By Belva's eighty-fifth birthday, women could vote in twelve states and the territory of Alaska.

On that eighty-fifth birthday, October 30, 1915, Belva made a speech. "Suffrage is no longer an issue," she declared, "it is an accomplished fact. Those states which have denied it to women will come around."

Achieving suffrage one state at a time was a long process. That's why the National Woman Suffrage Association and the National American Woman Suffrage Association had worked for a Constitutional amendment. The woman suffrage amendment had been introduced in every session of Congress since 1878. Each time, it had failed. Yet when Belva died at the age of eighty-six, on May 20, 1917, she was sure she had dedicated a great part of her lifetime to a goal that was nearly won. And Belva knew her lifelong efforts had been successful in other ways. Her fight for women's rights had exposed many of the injustices women suffered and had helped to correct some of these wrongs. Her law practice, work for peace, and presidential campaigns had shown doubters that women were as capable as men. "I have not raised the dead," she said near the end of her life, "but I have awakened the living."

The year after Belva's death, the House of Representatives endorsed a Constitutional amendment granting women the right to vote. The Senate passed the amendment in 1919, and sent it to the states for their approval. Suffragettes and other supporters worked frantically to get the required three-fourths of the states to ratify the amendment in time for the presidential election of 1920. Many states had special legislative sessions in order to vote on the amendment. On August 26, 1920, the secretary of state officially proclaimed that the Nineteenth Amendment had been approved by thirty-six of the forty-eight state legislatures. Three years after Belva's death, women across the nation had won the right to vote.

A large mountain had been moved, and Belva Lockwood was part of the force that moved it.

Afterword

Belva Lockwood was inducted into the National Women's Hall of Fame at Seneca Falls, New York, on July 16, 1983. A seventeen-cent U.S. postage stamp was issued in her honor on June 18, 1986. She is the thirtieth historic subject of the postal service's "Great American" series.

Girl Scouts in the area where Belva grew up take a special interest in her. Four troops in Middleport, New York, instituted a Belva A. Lockwood badge in the summer of 1975. In October 1984, the badge was made open to all Girl Scouts in Niagara County, New York. Some call themselves the "Belva Dears."

Belva had been called "Belva, dear" in the press during the 1888 campaign, when she and Alfred Love ran against Benjamin Harrison and Grover Cleveland. There was a seven-verse song about her written for the *Morning Journal* in Washington. This is the first verse:

> We'll not vote for Ben nor Grove,
> Belva, dear; Belva, dear;
> For our choice is you and "Love,"
> Belva, dear; Belva, dear;
> We endorse your views in full
> For we know you're sound on *wool*,
> With a husband's hair to pull,
> Belva, dear; Belva, dear;
> With a husband's hair to pull,
> Belva, dear; Belva, dear.

Belva Lockwood's struggle was for all of us—girls and boys, women and men. For when the lot of one part of our society is improved, we are all better for it. It's important to remember that many men worked for women's rights. All those votes which Belva received were votes cast by men.

Few women could vote in 1884, and only men could vote in national elections. (People who lived in territories could not vote for president.) One hundred years later, women voters outnumbered men. According to a release by the United States Census Bureau, women outvoted men for the first time in 1984. Seven million more women than men voted in the presidential election that year. Women don't vote as a bloc any more than men do, but the fact that they vote changes the way candidates look at the issues.

After I had begun my research on Belva, I discovered, to my amazement and delight, that my great-aunt was named for her. In 1886, between Belva Lockwood's two presidential campaigns, a little girl was born in the hills of West Virginia. Her father, my great-grandfather, named her Plina Belva Lockwood.

Grandpa Smith, as we called my great-grandfather, was active in politics in Lincoln County, West Virginia. Only one vote for Belva was recorded in the state in 1884, and that vote was cast in Logan County, not Lincoln County. But West Virginia, like Pennsylvania and some other states, has been known to have vote counters who threw away ballots. We don't know if that happened in the 1884 election, but I'm certain that if Grandpa's vote had been thrown away, someone in the family would have heard about it. It's probable that while Grandpa regarded Belva highly, he decided that his ballot would be worth more if he voted for one of the nominees from the established parties. Knowing Grandpa's politics, I'd guess he voted for Cleveland. But he must have greatly admired the woman lawyer who had the courage and confidence to run for president.

I didn't know Grandpa Smith very well, for he died when I was very young, but I couldn't escape the feeling that he was looking over my shoulder as I wrote this book.

Sources

Shortly after Geraldine Ferraro was nominated for vice president in 1984, *Boca Raton News* columnist Ann Gazourian wrote about the woman who had been nominated for president one hundred years earlier. Ms. Gazourian said she'd never heard of Belva Lockwood before. Neither had I.

Then the fun began.

I called on Herman Herst, a Boca Raton, Florida, resident who had given Ann the information about Belva. Mr. Herst is a *philatelist*, a person who collects and studies postage stamps. His interest in Belva had begun when the Town of Royalton Historical Society started its campaign to have a U.S. postal stamp dedicated to Belva. Along with a stack of newspaper clippings, Mr. Herst gave me the address of Norma Wollenberg of Gasport, New York, who was leading the fight for Belva's stamp.

I wrote to Mrs. Wollenberg, and she sent letters and newspaper articles from the stamp project. She also sent a book—*Belva A. Lockwood* by Julia Hull Winner (Niagara County Historical Society, 1969)—in which were reprinted Lura's newspaper columns, articles written about Belva during her lifetime, and some of Belva's manuscripts (including "My Efforts to Become a Lawyer"). Later, Mrs. Wollenberg sent copies of photographs and several letters handwritten by Belva on her letterhead stationery.

Letters, photographs, and contemporary newspaper and magazine articles are called *primary sources*. Other primary sources are diaries, interviews, and any writing—or even drawings—by the subject. People called *archivists* collect such primary source material and take special care of it. Historical societies have archivists, and their files are called *archives*. Many of the items Mrs. Wollenberg copied and sent are kept in the archives at the Royalton Historical Society.

For many famous people, archivists have stacks of boxes filled with letters, diaries, and other primary source material. Sometimes the boxes fill a room. But this is not true for Belva. She must have written and received many letters over her long and busy life; she must have made many notes as she prepared her cases and drafted her courtroom arguments. Perhaps she even kept a diary. But all this material has disappeared. Only small amounts exist here and there.

For example, the Swarthmore College Peace Collection has letters between Belva and Alfred Love. Swarthmore also has Belva's handwritten recollection of how the government attorney in the Cherokee case called her one of the most famous women lawyers in the country. Gleeson Library at the University of San Francisco has the handwritten contract between Belva and Jim Taylor dividing the fees earned in the Cherokee case. But for the most part, I had to turn to other sources—*secondary sources*.

The library is a good place to find secondary sources, such as books about the subject. Three library books about Belva helped me examine what her life must have been like. They were Terry Dunnahoo's *Before the Supreme Court* (Houghton Mifflin, 1974), Mary Virginia Fox's *Lady for the Defense* (Harcourt Brace Jovanovich, 1975), and Laura Kerr's *The Girl Who Ran for President* (Thomas Nelson, 1947). In these books, however, the authors often imagined what might have happened, weaving invented thoughts and conversations around the facts.

I also consulted *anthologies*, collections of stories or chapters which have the same theme. Two useful ones were Madeleine Stern's *We the Women: Career Firsts of Nineteenth-Century Americans* (Schulte, 1962), with the chapter "The First Woman Admitted to Practice Before the United States Supreme Court, Belva Ann Lockwood, 1879," and David Boynick's *Women Who Led the Way: Eight Pioneers for Equal Rights* (Crowell, 1972), with "Pioneering Attorney, Belva Ann Lockwood."

Sometimes old books which are no longer easily available are reprinted for present-day readers. An example of this is *History of Woman Suffrage*, edited between 1881 and 1922 by Elizabeth Cady Stanton, Susan B. Anthony, and Matilda Joslyn Gage. It was reprinted in 1969 by Arno (New York) in five fat volumes totaling almost five thousand pages. Eyewitness accounts of woman suffrage efforts and the status of women in each of the states fill these pages. There are speeches and reminiscences by famous women about their work for women's rights. Here one can find accounts of the seventy women who tried to vote in Washington, D.C., in 1871 and the events at the 1876 Centennial celebration.

Libraries also have collections of magazines. One especially helpful article was Julia Davis's "A Feisty Schoolmarm Made the Lawyers Sit Up and Take Notice" (*Smithsonian*, March 1981).

A researcher can also consult biographical dictionaries. I used two: *Notable American Women 1607–1950* and *Dictionary of American Biography*.

I used modern newspaper articles, such as "A Woman's Place" by Jacqui Salmon in the *Buffalo News Magazine* (April 3, 1983), but also read articles in different old newspapers by reporters who heard or interviewed Belva. Here, the *New York Times Index* was an important help. I looked for Belva Lockwood's name during the years of her struggle to be admitted to the Supreme Court and her tries for the presidency. Thus, I found an interview with Belva reported in the *New York Times* on October 19, 1884. In this interview, she revealed that Uriah's nickname for her was "Bell." No other source had this bit of information.

There was yet another source. Sarah Hull, the sister-in-law of the deceased historian Julia Hull Winner, telephoned me when she heard I was writing a book about Belva Lockwood. Mrs. Hull gave me two other Belva Lockwood books by her sister-in-law. And since she had grown up in Gasport, she was able to tell me about the farms and mills in the area.

Researching a person's life is like working on a jigsaw puzzle. With this kind of puzzle, however, there are many pieces of information that won't fit into the book. Some pieces are found to be untrue and must be thrown away. Other pieces must be left out because of limited space. Deciding what to omit is as difficult as deciding what to put in. And where, exactly, will all the "in" pieces fit to make the biography the most interesting for the reader?

Deciding is part of writing.